# Hedgehugs
## Horace and Hattiepillar

Horace and Hattie are
the very best of friends.

There are so many things they like to do together.

They like to watch blossom fall from the trees.

They like to look for the first star of the night.

They like to play hide and seek in the meadow.

And on clear nights they try to catch the moon.

When Horace is busy, Hattie practises handstands among the dandelion clocks.

When Hattie is busy, Horace climbs to the top of his favourite tree.

Horace and Hattie are the
very best of friends.

One day they found something tiny and interesting under a leaf.

It was small and shiny and smooth.

Then out crawled a wriggly, stripy thing.

It looked at Horace and Hattie.

Then it started to eat.

In no time at all the leaf was gone.

Horace and Hattie found it more leaves.

It ate and ate. It got bigger and **bigger**.

...and **bigger**

...and **bigger**.

Then, one day it stopped eating.

It made a soft,
silky bed, and
there it slept ...

...for lots of days ...

...and lots of nights.

Then one sunny morning
the little bed opened up.

Out crawled something
beautiful, colourful
and wonderful.

It looked at Horace and Hattie,
waved its wings...

...then fluttered away.

Horace had an idea.

If they ate lots and slept in a soft, silky bed, maybe they would turn into something beautiful, colourful and wonderful too.

Hattie munched.

Horace crunched.

They ate until their tummies were all full up.

They scooped and gathered and collected until they had a fluffy bed of flowers.

Horace and Hattie nestled in the petals . . .

...and they drifted off to sleep.

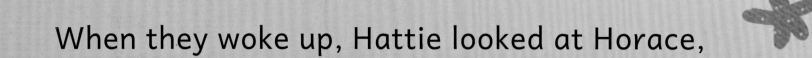

When they woke up, Hattie looked at Horace,

Horace looked at Hattie. Had they changed?

Yes!

They were beautiful,
colourful
and wonderful!

...And they even managed to fly too!

The End

'Hedgehugs – Horace and Hattiepillar'
An original concept by Lucy Tapper and Steve Wilson
© Lucy Tapper and Steve Wilson
Written by Lucy Tapper and Steve Wilson
Illustrated by Lucy Tapper

Published by MAVERICK ARTS PUBLISHING LTD
Studio 3A, City Business Centre, 6 Brighton Road, Horsham, West Sussex, RH13 5BB
© Maverick Arts Publishing Limited  +44 (0)1403 256941

Published May 2015

A CIP catalogue record for this book is available at the British Library.

ISBN 978-1-84886-163-3

**Maverick**
arts publishing
www.maverickbooks.co.uk

## Hedgehugs - Lovingly created by Lucy Tapper & Steve Wilson

Lucy Tapper is an illustrator, artist and designer. She loves all things beautiful and likes to surround herself with wild flowers, pretty fabrics and colour. Lucy is the creative force behind www.fromlucy.com.

Steve Wilson is Lucy's business partner at FromLucy and has a long history in children's TV presenting and writing music, hence his love of words, stories and characters.

Steve and Lucy live in a little cottage in Devon with their two daughters Daisy and Holly.